Lydia Jane and the Baby-Sitter Exchange

Lydia Jane and the Baby-Sitter Exchange

by Natalie Honeycutt

Bradbury Press • New York

Maxwell Macmillan Canada • Toronto
Maxwell Macmillan International
New York • Oxford • Singapore • Sydney

Bradbury Press
Macmillan Publishing Company
866 Third Avenue
New York, NY 10022

Maxwell Macmillan Canada, Inc.
1200 Eglinton Avenue East
Suite 200
Don Mills, Ontario M3C 3N1

Macmillan Publishing Company is part of the Maxwell Communication
Group of Companies.

First edition
Printed and bound in the United States of America
10 9 8 7 6 5 4 3 2 1

The text of this book is set in 14 pt. Zapf International Light.
Library of Congress Cataloging-in-Publication Data
Honeycutt, Natalie.
Lydia Jane and the baby-sitter exchange.—1st ed.
p. cm.
Summary: Eight-year-old Lydia Jane, dissatisfied with her highly cautious
baby-sitter and her rules, hatches several plots to liberate herself
from the stifling situation.
ISBN 0-02-744362-0
[1. Babysitters—Fiction. 2. Family life—Fiction.] I. Title.
PZ7.H7467Ly 1993
[Fic]—dc20 92-46363

For Bunny and Randy,
who waited patiently
by the shores of Moses Lake

Lydia Jane and the
Baby-Sitter Exchange

Chapter

1

"*I can't believe she made me miss it,*" Lydia Jane said. It was Tuesday, and she and Gabrielle were on their way home from Mrs. Humphrey's house.

"Mrs. Humphrey is the worst sitter in Westmont," said Lydia Jane. "She's probably the worst sitter in the entire world."

Gabrielle didn't answer. She was busy duck-walking along the parking strip, gathering plum blossom petals as she went. She dropped the petals, two and five at a time, into the bib pocket of her coveralls.

Lydia Jane didn't mind that Gabrielle wasn't listening. She wasn't talking to her little sister anyhow. Lydia Jane was practicing. She was getting ready for what she was going to say to her parents as soon as she got home.

"Mrs. Humphrey is ruining my life!" Lydia Jane said. "You don't want your oldest daughter's whole life ruined, do you?"

Mrs. Humphrey had been Lydia Jane's after-school baby-sitter for more than two months. And she was Gabrielle's all-day baby-sitter—Gabrielle was just four years old, and too young for regular school.

For two months, Mrs. Humphrey had said no to everything Lydia Jane wanted to do that was interesting or fun. As far as Lydia Jane could tell, *no* was Mrs. Humphrey's favorite word.

Lydia Jane longed to be back at Happy Times Day Care where Mrs. Martin let children do whatever they wanted. And she missed being around other kids. Like Mindy Rufkin, who was her own age and also in Mrs. Lacey's third grade class at Mills Elementary School.

Lydia Jane had even started to miss that six-year-old toad, Acey Pleever. Though the way Lydia Jane saw it, Acey was the whole reason she and Gabrielle had to leave Happy Times Day Care in the first place.

It had happened on the day Acey made up a game called Horror Movie. First he chased a girl around the yard with a pair of scissors. Then, when he caught her, Acey handed over the scissors and the girl chased him. Screaming was a big part of the game. The person being chased was supposed to scream the entire time.

Gabrielle hadn't been playing because she was busy with a coloring book. And Lydia Jane hadn't been playing because she thought it was a stupid game. Besides, she was watching a spider build a web. It was a big, loose, lopsided web, with holes large enough to put a foot through, and Lydia Jane was trying to decide whether it was the spider's first web, and how it would ever catch dinner in *that* when her mother arrived, right in the middle of all the screaming and chasing, to pick up her girls. Mrs. Bly took one look, grabbed Gabrielle and

Lydia Jane each by a hand, and they left Happy Times Day Care for good.

"That irresponsible woman!" Mrs. Bly had said about Mrs. Martin. "She'll be lucky if someone doesn't get killed."

The scissors, as Lydia Jane had reminded her mother a dozen times over, had round tips. They were plastic. Red plastic.

For two days, Mrs. Bly stayed home from work and telephoned day-care centers and baby-sitters. She asked each a list of questions about supervision and safety. And scissors. And then she found Mrs. Humphrey.

"I hate going there!" Lydia Jane said. Then to Gabrielle she said, "Come on, let's hurry."

Gabrielle looked up at Lydia Jane through a fringe of curly red hair—hair exactly like Lydia Jane's own—and blinked. "But you say *not* to hurry," Gabrielle said. "You say to go slow and look."

"That's true," Lydia Jane said. "Grandma always says you can't learn anything unless you take time to look." And her grandmother should know, Lydia Jane thought. She had been a college science professor until she retired.

4

"But today's different," Lydia Jane said. "We have to hurry today because the sooner we get home, the sooner Mom can start phoning for a different sitter."

Gabrielle peered into the pocket of her bib overalls. "It's not full," she said. Her lower lip drooped.

Lydia Jane sighed. She stooped in the parking strip by Gabrielle and gathered petals as fast as she could. Then, when Gabrielle's pocket was full, she took her by the hand and led her home.

As they rounded the corner onto Washoe Court, Lydia Jane's heart danced a step of pleasure. No matter what kind of mood she was in, seeing her home never failed to make her feel better.

Lydia Jane Bly thought she lived in the luckiest spot in all of Westmont, California. Lucky because the Bly cottage was on the border of a large wooded lot. At the very back of the lot was a creek. And beyond the creek were still more woods, then the edge of McKinley Park. To Lydia Jane, it seemed that her family had an entire forest of their very own.

And of course, the best thing about living at the edge of a forest was all the animals *in* the forest. Like the squirrels. And a pair of ravens whose nest Lydia Jane had found. And the family of raccoons that had moved into the crawl space beneath the Bly's very own house.

Lydia Jane and Gabrielle both walked faster as they neared the cottage. They turned in at the hedge and walked up the flagstone path by the driveway. Their parents' cars were parked one behind the other. Lydia Jane and Gabrielle walked past the cars and up the wooden steps to the side door.

Inside the cottage, Lydia Jane smelled onions frying on the stove. She could hear her parents laughing. She dropped Gabrielle's hand. Then she dropped her backpack on the floor. Both of them streaked for the kitchen.

"Our troops have returned!" Mr. Bly said. He scooped Gabrielle up in his arms, while Mrs. Bly clasped Lydia Jane in a hug.

"Boy, am I ever glad to see you," Mrs. Bly said. She said the same thing every day, but she always sounded like she meant it.

"Don't squash me," Gabrielle said. "I have something." She squirmed to the floor, then dug into her bib pocket.

"You'll never guess what happened today," Lydia Jane said.

"What?" asked her parents, both at once.

"It hailed!" Lydia Jane said.

"I noticed that," her mother said. "It hailed in Roytown, too." Roytown was where Mrs. Bly worked.

"It didn't hail in the city," her father said. "But then, I didn't have much time to look out the windows."

"Petals!" Gabrielle said. She strewed a handful of petals across the kitchen table. "The hail made them. It knocked the flowers right off the trees!"

"And I missed it!" Lydia Jane said. "It hailed today and I completely missed it! Mrs. Humphrey wouldn't let me go outside, so I had to watch it hail through the window. Do you believe that?"

"She can't believe she missed it," Gabrielle said.

"That's a shame," Mr. Bly said.

"You must have been very disappointed," Mrs. Bly said.

"I was," Lydia Jane said. "And all because of Mrs. Humphrey. All she thinks about is safety, safety, safety."

Lydia Jane's father leaned back against the kitchen counter. He crossed his feet at the ankles. He folded his arms. "I thought we were talking about hail," he said. "It sounds like this is shaping up to be a complaint about Mrs. Humphrey."

"*Another* complaint," her mother said. She leaned back against the kitchen counter, too. She crossed her ankles. She folded her arms.

"You have to understand," Lydia Jane said. "My whole life I have waited to see hail. *Real* hail, not just on TV. And when it finally comes, I'm at Mrs. Humphrey's house and she won't let me out!"

"Your whole life?" her father said. "Let's see, that's eight years, right?"

"Eight years, nine months," her mother said. "My bathing suit is older than that."

"But it was my whole, *entire* life," Lydia

Jane said. "And anyway, *you* would have let me out. Anyone would have let me out. Except Mrs. Humphrey."

"That depends," Mr. Bly said. "How big was the hail?"

"I've seen hail as big as baseballs," Mrs. Bly said.

"Marbles," Lydia Jane said. "It was the same size as marbles."

"It bounced," Gabrielle said. She was arranging petals on the table in little clumps of five each. They looked like flowers.

"I suppose we'd have let you out in marble-sized hail," Mr. Bly said. "But then what would you have done?"

"I'd have looked at it," Lydia Jane said. "I'd have caught some in my hand and looked to see if it was smooth or bumpy. I'd have looked inside, in case I could see *stuff* in there. I'd stomp on some to see how it breaks. I'd lick it to see how it tastes."

"Just like my mother," Mrs. Bly said with a smile. "The soul of a scientist . . ."

"I'd put some in a jar so I could study it later," Lydia Jane went on. "I could put it in the freezer and then melt one piece at a time and look at it under my microscope. Maybe something would be swimming around and it would be a new kind of germ from space and I could discover it!"

"Jars can break," Gabrielle said. "Mrs. Humphrey said so."

"She wouldn't even let me have a jar to catch some in!" Lydia Jane said. "The chance of a lifetime down the drain."

"More likely down the gutters," her father said. He didn't look nearly as upset as Lydia Jane had expected him to.

"I'm sure Mrs. Humphrey just didn't want you to be hurt," Mrs. Bly said. "After all, she knows the kinds of things that can happen to children. She raised four of her own, you know."

Lydia Jane tried to imagine Mrs. Humphrey as somebody's mother. She couldn't.

"I'll bet they all ran away," she said.

"There are worse things than missing a hailstorm," her father said.

"I know," Lydia Jane said. "Like I could miss a meteorite! If a meteorite fell in Mrs.

Humphrey's yard, she'd probably pull the shades and call the police. I'd never see it! That would be even worse than missing hail."

"I don't think that's what your father meant," Mrs. Bly said.

"But it's what *I* meant," Lydia Jane said. She was coming to the important part now. "I can't *do* things at Mrs. Humphrey's. I can't do experiments, and I can't find things out. I'll never figure out how anything works. And if I can't figure out how anything works, I'll never be able to patch the hole in the ozone layer. I want to go back to Happy Times Day Care."

"Me, too," Gabrielle said. "Lydia Jane hates Mrs. Humphrey's house, and so do I!"

Mrs. Bly sighed. "I think this was a complaint about Mrs. Humphrey," she said.

"A major complaint," Mr. Bly said.

Lydia Jane's parents looked at each other. They didn't talk, they just looked. It suddenly struck Lydia Jane that her parents looked like twins. Except that one was a little taller than the other. And the tall one had brown hair, and the other had red hair. Except for that, Lydia Jane thought, they looked exactly like twins. Stubborn twins.

"Your mother and I need to talk," Mr. Bly said at last, "so why don't you girls go find something to do."

"Homework would be good," Mrs. Bly said. She looked at Lydia Jane when she said it.

Lydia Jane sighed. This was probably not a good time to remind her parents that there were more interesting things in life than homework.

She retrieved her backpack from the living room, then walked down the short hall to the room she shared with Gabrielle. Two chests of drawers, each facing the opposite direction, made a kind of central divider in the room. It wasn't exactly the same as having rooms of their own, but it would have to do for now. Lydia Jane's parents had spent weekends for the last six months converting their attached garage into a room that would one day be Lydia Jane's.

Not that Lydia Jane minded sharing with Gabrielle. She didn't. But Gabrielle and

Lydia Jane were both growing, and their room seemed to get smaller each year. Lydia Jane looked forward to the day when she could spread out.

She tossed her backpack on her bed and flopped on her belly beside it. She unzipped it cautiously and peeked inside. There were papers inside in various states of disrepair, and the edge of a workbook or two.

She slid her hand into the bottom of the backpack. Some things she could identify, and some she couldn't. There were pencils. Those were easy. And some eraser ends. And a chain she had picked up from the playground. And one of those balls that looks like it's made of rubber hair. But there were other things that Lydia Jane couldn't identify by touch. Her backpack became more mysterious by the week. When she dumped it out at the end of the school year, she'd find lots of nice surprises.

Lydia Jane pulled out a chewed pencil and her math workbook. She turned to the page of problems she was supposed to solve, and glanced over it.

She stuck the pencil in her mouth and

gnawed lightly. Most of the math problems looked easy. And boring. But there were two that looked hard. Lydia Jane concentrated on these and worked them out as best she could. Then she closed the book and shoved it back in her backpack.

"Done," she said aloud.

Lydia Jane propped herself on one elbow and looked around her half-room. What to do? She could pick up the clothes that were scattered everywhere. But on the other hand, some of the clothes were hardly dirty and could be worn again. And the others were such nice colors. Lydia Jane liked bright colors. It was cheerful to see patches of fuchsia, neon green, and electric orange dotted about.

She made her way across the room to the shelves by the window where she kept her experiments. Jars of mold sat on the shelves. Mostly, the molds were from things that her mother hadn't quite gotten around to cleaning out of the refrigerator. Lydia Jane had put bits of moldy cheese and fruits and casseroles into separate jars and was watching them grow.

"Wow," she said. A jar that had had less than an inch of mold the day before was now nearly full to the top.

"Come see this, Gabrielle," she said. "It's amazing."

Gabrielle's voice came from somewhere on the other side of the chests of drawers. "I'm busy," she said.

"Doing what?" Lydia Jane asked.

"I'm being a petal princess," Gabrielle called.

Lydia Jane shrugged. She settled down in front of the jar of mold. If the mold had grown three inches in one day, she could probably *see* it growing if she tried. She intended to try.

Forty minutes later, she was still trying when she heard her father call, "Lydia Jane, Gabrielle, dinner!"

And that's when the entire family got to find out what a petal princess looked like.

Pink plum-blossom petals were stuck to every inch of Gabrielle. Every inch within reach of her small hands, that is. Which meant nearly everywhere. From her shoes to her hair.

"The petal princess comes in the spring!" she said.

"Awesome," Lydia Jane said.

Mrs. Bly buried her face in her hands.

Mr. Bly doubled over with laughter.

Gabrielle twirled around, showering fistfuls of petals as she turned.

"Gabrielle, how did you do this?" Mrs. Bly asked.

"Glue!" Gabrielle said.

"Oh, no . . ."

"It's not glue," Lydia Jane said. "It can't be. You hid all the glue, remember? It must be paste."

"Thank goodness," her mother said. "Paste washes out. Glue doesn't."

For some reason this made Lydia Jane's father laugh all the harder. "Well, that makes it all right then," he bellowed. "That makes everything just dandy. Har-de-har-har." Then, "Don't you see, honey? This is a perfect example of what we were just talking about. Children need watching."

"Especially ours," Mrs. Bly said. She shook her head.

Lydia Jane's heart sank. She knew what was coming.

And it came. During dinner. In a long lecture in which her parents told her all of the reasons why safety was more important than hailstones.

In bed that night, Lydia Jane listened as the petal princess, freshly bathed, hummed herself to sleep. Lydia Jane wanted to say, "This is your fault. If you hadn't put paste in your hair, Mom would be on the phone right now finding a new sitter." But she knew her parents' minds had already been made up. If anyone was to blame, it was probably Acey Pleever.

As Lydia Jane drifted toward sleep, she thought about plum blossoms and paste. And glue. And then she thought of someone else who might be partly to blame. Because the reason her parents had hidden the glue in the first place had to do with Cheerios . . . and with Lydia Jane herself.

Chapter

2

*A*t *7:45 the next morning, while Lydia* Jane stood on a stool in front of the bathroom mirror brushing her hair, her mother came in, followed by Gabrielle. Mrs. Bly was dressed as she was each morning, in crisp denim coveralls and white running shoes. She wore large, metallic pink, moon-shaped earrings, a freshly pressed pink kerchief knotted carefully around her neck, and pink lipstick.

Lydia Jane thought her mother looked beautiful. Mrs. Bly said she thought it was important to look nice even if you worked at a job where you wore coveralls. "I like to be a credit to my trade," she said. Lydia Jane's mother was a welder.

Mr. Bly had already left for his job in the city, where he worked as a cost accountant for a construction company. He said his job was mostly to add up numbers all day, which Lydia Jane thought sounded dreadful, but which her father seemed to like. He'd gone around the breakfast table kissing everyone good-bye. "My passel of redheads," he called them, sounding, as always, as though he had just won a free trip to Hawaii.

"I have to leave now," Lydia Jane's mother said from the bathroom door. "I don't want to get caught in traffic and be late to work."

"I know," Lydia Jane said. Every morning her mother said the same thing. Next she would apologize for leaving Lydia Jane to get herself off to school.

"I'm sorry I can't stay to see you off," her mother said, "but I have to drop Gabrielle off at Mrs. Humphrey's."

"It's okay," Lydia Jane said. "I don't mind, really."

Gabrielle edged around their mother to give Lydia Jane a good-bye kiss.

"Good luck, kid," Lydia Jane said.

"Bye, Lyddie," Gabrielle said.

Lydia Jane picked up the can of mousse and gave it a good shake.

"Your lunch is by the door," her mother said. "Don't forget to take it."

"I won't," Lydia Jane said. She squeezed a heap of white foam into one hand.

"And remember to pull the door hard. . . ."

"So it will latch," Lydia Jane said. She was never quite certain whether her mother thought she couldn't remember these things, or if she just enjoyed repeating her-self. Lydia Jane smeared the mousse on ex-actly half of her hair.

"And take good care of Gabrielle on the way home today," her mother said.

"I will," Lydia Jane said. "I always do."

"Well, then, I guess that's all." Mrs. Bly wrapped her arms around Lydia Jane and squeezed. "Good-bye, sweetie."

"Bye, Mom," Lydia Jane said. She was careful not to smear mousse on her mother when she hugged back.

At the bathroom door, Mrs. Bly stopped and turned back. "Oh, and Lydia Jane," she said, "do please try not to be late to school. You have plenty of time, and if you keep your eye on the clock there really is no reason to be tardy."

"Okay," Lydia Jane said. "I'll try."

When her mother was gone, Lydia Jane slicked back the moussed side of her hair until it clung like plastic wrap to her head. Then she brushed the other half until it frizzed up in all directions. She smiled at the result. Lydia Jane was always happy when she could think up some new way to give her hair attitude.

Next she went into her bedroom and rummaged among the clutter on her dresser until she found two earrings. One was a tiny green frog, and the other was a silver star. She put these in her ears, then shoved the laces into her black high-tops and pulled them on. Then she got her backpack, picked up her lunch box by the side door, and left the house. She pulled the door until she heard it latch.

Lydia Jane stood on the steps and looked around. Her mother was right. There was really no reason to be late to school. Then again, as Lydia Jane saw it, there was really no reason to be on time, either.

She walked around the back of the cottage and along the north wall until she came to the hole that led to the crawl space under the cottage.

Lydia Jane knelt and peered into the darkness. "Are you guys in there?" she called. Because she had only heard the raccoons at night, Lydia Jane wasn't positive that they spent their days under the cottage. But she also knew that raccoons are nocturnal. They were probably under there sleeping—all worn out from a night of roaming and fighting and tipping over garbage cans.

Still, Lydia Jane wished they'd come out in the daytime so she could get a good look at them. She'd like to know just how many there were, and if any were pregnant. Maybe there were babies already.

Lydia Jane rested her chin in her hands and thought. If she could at least see their footprints, she could tell how big they were. . . .

Then she had an idea.

Lydia Jane unlooped the garden hose from where it hung coiled on its rack, turned on the spigot, then dragged the hose back to the entrance to the crawl space. For a long time she stood there, letting water soak into the bare ground in front of the entry. From time to time she poked her fingers into the deepening mud. When finally it felt just right, she turned off the water, fetched a length of two-by-four from the pile of scrap lumber by the garage, and ran the edge of the board lightly across the mud. She stroked carefully, working slowly back and forth the way she'd seen workmen smooth cement for a sidewalk.

At last she was done. She wiped her hands on her shirttail and looked with satisfaction at her mudflat. It was mirror smooth. Anything that walked across it would leave a clear track.

By the time Lydia Jane walked into Room 4 of Mills Elementary School, she was late. Sharing was over. All the kids had cursive workbooks open on their desks.

Lydia Jane plopped into her seat on one side of the double desk she shared with Juliet Fisher.

Once upon a time, Lydia Jane would have said Juliet was the biggest pain in the whole class. She always did everything perfectly, and she announced other people's mistakes. But lately, Juliet had begun to change. Sometimes she made mistakes of her own, and she laughed and talked more and tried new things. Much to Lydia Jane's surprise, she had found herself liking Juliet. And it was fun to show her things. Like how to put all your spelling words in only three sentences. Or how to slide into second base. This weekend she had promised to teach Juliet how to roller-skate. Juliet Fisher was almost Lydia Jane's very best friend.

"I'm late," Lydia Jane said.

"I know," Juliet said. "I was late yesterday, remember."

"I had to make an experiment," Lydia Jane explained. "I'll tell you about it if it works."

"Great," Juliet said. Then she said, "We're supposed to work on the letter X. Mrs. Lacy says we'll finish Y and Z next week. Z looks weird in cursive. It doesn't look like the kind of letter a zebra would use at all, do you think?"

Lydia Jane plowed through the contents of her desk until she came up with her cursive workbook and a pencil. "No, it doesn't," she agreed. She turned to the X page and made a quick line of cursive Xs. Then she closed the book. "Done," she said.

"Me, too," Juliet said. She had completed two and a half of the five lines provided. She closed her book.

"Do you want to make constellations?" Lydia Jane asked. "See, I have all these sticky-backed, glow-in-the-dark stars, and when my new room is done I'm going to put them all over the ceiling. So I was thinking I could do things like the Big Dipper and Orion's Belt.

"Then I got to thinking, why do the same

old boring constellations you can see all the time? Why not dream up some new ones?"

"Good idea," Juliet said. "How do we do it?"

"You just need paper," Lydia Jane said.

Juliet opened her binder, which was not as neat as it used to be, and yanked out several sheets of blank paper. She handed one to Lydia Jane.

"First you choose what to do," Lydia Jane explained. "I'm doing a raccoon. Then maybe a newt. First you draw the outline." She bent over her paper and drew the outline of a raccoon in profile. She wasn't sure the ears were placed right, but they were good enough.

Juliet watched for a few minutes. Then she said, "I think I'll do an elephant seal. I got to really liking them when I had to do that stupid report." She was talking about reports the class had done on animal habitats. Juliet had done a habitat report on elephant seals with Granville Jones and Jonah Twist.

"Good idea," Lydia Jane said. "I like elephant seals, too."

For a time both girls worked in silence. Lydia Jane tried out three different raccoon drawings. The one she liked showed the raccoon stuffing food into its mouth.

She looked into her desk for a paper clip. She didn't find one, but she did find a mechanical pencil that had lost its lead.

"Now," she said, "watch this."

At several points along the outline of the raccoon, Lydia Jane poked holes. She poked one at the tip of the nose and at each foot, two along the back, and three at the tip of the tail.

"There," she said. She handed the paper to Juliet. "Now hold it up toward the window and look."

Juliet held the paper up. Several pinpoints of bright light shone through, just like stars. "That's great," she said.

"Isn't it?" Lydia Jane agreed. "Of course it would be better on black paper. Then the paper would look more like space. Did you know that the thing about space is that it isn't space at all?"

"How can space not be space?" Juliet asked.

"It's just not," Lydia Jane said. "Most of space isn't really empty at all. It just looks like it is because we can only see the stars. But the rest of space is full of *stuff*. Stuff nobody can see. But it's out there."

"Wow," Juliet said.

"Yeah," Lydia Jane said. "But I figure, even if I can't see it, I can still look at it. Like at night if I look at the stars, I only look at the stars a little while. The rest of the time I look at the space in between the stars. So even when it seems like I'm looking at nothing, I'm really looking at something. Get it?"

Juliet laughed. "Sort of," she said. "But it's a little weird."

"Try it," Lydia Jane said. "Some night just look at the space in between the stars. You'll be looking at most of the stuff space is made out of."

During the rest of cursive time, and during most of math time except when they were correcting homework (Lydia Jane's two problems were right), Lydia Jane and Juliet worked on new constellations. Lydia Jane finished the raccoon and a newt and a three-toed sloth. Juliet finished the elephant seal and a family of rabbits.

At recess time, they took their constellations outside and showed them to the other kids. Pretty soon everyone wanted to make new constellations.

"I'd make a unicorn," Mindy said.

Granville, wearing his usual outfit of camouflage clothes, said, "I'd make a UFO. Or maybe a stealth bomber."

Jonah said, "I'd make anything except a hamster. Hamsters are more trouble than you'd believe."

Juliet told everyone what Lydia Jane had said about the stuff in space.

"How do you know something's there if you can't see it?" Sara asked.

"Think of meteoroids," Lydia Jane said. "There are plenty of meteoroids right near Earth, and we can't see them."

As soon as she said that, she remembered about Mrs. Humphrey. "And with my luck, if one ever lands, I'll never get to see it," she said. She told everyone about the hail and about how Mrs. Humphrey had made her miss it. And about how her parents wouldn't get a new sitter because they thought safety was more important than hail.

"I don't have a sitter," Jonah said. "I just let myself in our house with a key. Then my brother, Todd, comes home from junior high school and he takes care of me. Supposedly. But mostly he bugs me." Jonah's shoulders sagged.

"I have Gabrielle, though," Lydia Jane said. "She's little, so she needs a sitter, and my parents think we should be together." She didn't mention that her parents thought she needed watching.

"My mom stays home," Granville said. "She says no one else would put up with me. Maybe your mother could quit work and stay home."

"She'd never do that," Lydia Jane said. "My mom's a welder, and she loves her job. She's always saying she'd go crazy if she couldn't go to work."

"If Mrs. Humphrey moved away, maybe your parents would send you back to Happy Times Day Care," Mindy said.

"I don't think she's going to move," Lydia Jane said. "She's not the kind of person who would do something new."

"You never can tell," Mindy said. "I have an aunt who all of a sudden packed up and moved to a place called Weed. Nobody has ever figured out why."

Juliet had been frowning down at her feet while everyone else was talking. Now she spoke up.

"I know what you need," she said. "You need an au pair. My cousins live in Mill Valley and they have an au pair. They think she's wonderful."

"What's an au pair?" Lydia Jane asked. Just offhand she thought it sounded like a tropical fruit. Not that that was so bad. A tropical fruit would be a better sitter than Mrs. Humphrey.

"It's a kind of baby-sitter who lives in your house. My cousins' au pair drives them to school and picks them up after. She takes them to the dentist and to Great America. And any time my aunt and uncle go out, they don't even have to call a sitter, because the au pair is always right there. She's from Finland, and she's pretty."

"What a great idea!" Lydia Jane said. Right off she could think of about sixteen different places she'd like her au pair to take her, starting with the San Francisco Planetarium and the Lawrence Hall of Science. And if Gabrielle wanted to go to the petting zoo, that would be okay, too.

"Just one thing," Lydia Jane said. "Is your cousins' au pair afraid of hail?"

"I don't think so," Juliet said. "But I think au pairs come in all kinds. You probably just ask for the kind you want."

"Fine, then," Lydia Jane said. "I know what kind I want. I'll get an au pair that's not afraid of hail or meteorites. I'll have one that isn't afraid of slimy things that live under rocks, or fuzzy things that grow in jars."

The more Lydia Jane thought about the sort of au pair she'd get, the happier she felt. She held her raccoon constellation to the sky and looked at it.

"I think I'll make a constellation that looks

like my au pair," she said. "It will have about twenty stars, and it will be very pretty. It will be a very special constellation."

A picture of the constellation began to form in Lydia Jane's mind. It got better with every passing moment.

"I'll even give it a name," she said at last. "I'll call it The Brave Au Pair."

Chapter

3

*O*n *Friday after school, Lydia Jane* walked up Mrs. Humphrey's front walk and rang the bell. It had been a long week. Lydia Jane had decided to wait until the weekend to tell her parents about the au pair.

On weekday evenings, Lydia Jane's parents were often tired. Sometimes, Lydia Jane believed, her parents said no to a perfectly good idea just because yes could mean a little extra effort. She'd hate to lose her brave au pair just because her parents were pooped.

The door swung open and Mrs. Humphrey stood there, smiling down at Lydia Jane. She had on a flowered dress, and a tan apron that started just under her chin and ended below her hem. Her eyebrows arched in black lines over her glasses in a way that gave her a startled look. Lydia Jane often puzzled over how Mrs. Humphrey could smile and look alarmed all at once.

"Why, Lydia Jane," she said, "I thought that was you. It was getting to be about that time."

"It's me," Lydia Jane said. She wanted to add, "But it won't be next time, because today's my last day." But she didn't say that. She didn't want Mrs. Humphrey to mention the au pair to her parents before she mentioned her herself.

"Come on through to the kitchen," Mrs. Humphrey said. "Your snack is waiting."

Lydia Jane followed Mrs. Humphrey through the living room. It wasn't like the living rooms that Lydia Jane was used to. There were no jackets tossed on the couch. No stacks of magazines and open bills on the coffee table. No stray pencils, toys, shoes, or coffee cups scattered about. It made Lydia Jane think of the rooms in museums. The ones with the velvet ropes across the doorways that meant you couldn't go in.

Gabrielle exploded out of the den and threw herself at Lydia Jane. "Lyddie's here!" she said. "Come play, Lyddie. I waited and waited."

Lydia Jane knew the rules. "I know," she said, "but I have to wash up and have my snack first. Then I can play."

Gabrielle's face fell. "I have to watch 'Flintstones,' huh?"

"Or something," Lydia Jane said. "I'll be there soon."

Gabrielle gave Lydia Jane a baleful look, then turned back to the den.

Lydia Jane knew that if she wanted to, she could skip the snack. But she couldn't skip the part about getting washed up. Mrs. Humphrey didn't like dirt on children. And she liked it even less in her house.

Lydia Jane stood on tiptoes to turn on the kitchen faucet. Then she used the bar of green soap and lathered all the way to her elbows. Over and over she rubbed her hands. When the suds were all brown, she ran her hands and arms under the warm running water. Then she picked up the folded white hand towel that lay on the counter and dried herself off.

Mrs. Humphrey stood nearby for inspection. She looked Lydia Jane up and down and shook her head. "Your face could use washing, too, young lady," she said.

"But I don't touch things with my face," Lydia Jane said. Sometimes Mrs. Humphrey made her wash her face, and sometimes she didn't.

"I guess we'll let it go this time," Mrs. Humphrey said. "But goodness, Lydia Jane, I can't imagine what they do with children in school these days. You are always covered in grime. I'm sure your mother doesn't allow you to leave the house like that in the morning."

Lydia Jane shrugged. "Maybe dirt likes me," she said.

"It must," Mrs. Humphrey said. "Why,

your shoes are even muddy, and it hasn't rained in over two days. You'd better let me have them."

Lydia Jane sat down at the kitchen table and took off her shoes. She handed them to Mrs. Humphrey. Then she picked up a peanut-butter-covered Ritz cracker from the plate and popped it carefully into her mouth. She kept her fingers away from the peanut butter. If she got any on her hands, she'd have to wash again.

Mrs. Humphrey stood over the wastebasket banging Lydia Jane's shoes together at the soles. Dried mud rained down into the trash. It happened to be mud that Lydia Jane was well acquainted with. It had come from her own backyard.

Lydia Jane's raccoon footprint experiment was a failure. So far. The problem, she thought, was that the mud dried too fast. By the time the raccoons came out, it was too hard for prints. But now that she had figured out what was wrong, she thought she could fix it.

Somehow, Lydia Jane did not believe that

the mudprint experiment was the sort of thing that would interest Mrs. Humphrey. So she kept this to herself.

When she had finished her peanut-buttered crackers and her milk, Lydia Jane set her dishes in the sink. Mrs. Humphrey was already washing them before she left the room.

Lydia Jane walked back to the den. The den was the only room Mrs. Humphrey liked children to play in. "There's nothing in here that can hurt you," she said. "So long as you don't roughhouse."

The way Lydia Jane had it figured, there was nothing in the den, period. There was an old brown-and-yellow flowered sofa, which Mrs. Humphrey kept covered with a sheet. And seven stuffed animals, and a Fisher-Price circus. And a beach ball you had to keep blowing up. And a TV.

Gabrielle was on the floor in front of the TV. The stuffed animals were gathered around her, facing the screen. She held a remote control in her hands and punched a button with her thumb.

"News," she said. "Cartoons. Wrestling. Cooking. War. Cartoons. Music. Things to buy. Weather. Kissing. Commercials. Commercials. Baseball. News. Lions. Cartoons. Talking."

"What are you watching?" Lydia Jane asked.

Gabrielle looked up. "Everything," she said. She punched another button. "Nothing!" The screen went black. "Let's play Parachute," she said.

"Can't," Lydia Jane said. Parachute was a game she'd made up using the sheet and the sofa. Parachutes, Lydia Jane knew, made gravity work slower. It was a pretty simple game. You jumped off the sofa holding the sheet over your head. Then you fell in a heap. It didn't do much to slow down gravity, but it was fun.

Gabrielle loved it.

Mrs. Humphrey said to stop. Someone could break a leg.

Lydia Jane kept coming up with new games. The more interesting the game, the less Mrs. Humphrey seemed to like it.

"I know what we can do," she said. "We can be bats. I found this book about bats in the library. It told how bats use sonar for flying around in the dark. They make a high humming sound, and then the sound bounces off things and comes right back to the bats' ears. The bat can tell where everything is, just from the way the sound bounces."

"I want to be a bat," Gabrielle said. She bounced up and down. "Let's be bats."

"Okay," Lydia Jane said, "but you have to close your eyes so it will be dark. No peeking."

Gabrielle squeezed her eyes shut tight.

"Now hum," Lydia Jane said.

Gabrielle hummed "Row, Row, Row Your Boat."

"Not a tune," Lydia Jane said. "Just hum plain. One note. Like this. Hmmmmmmm mmmmmmmmmmmmmmmmmmmmmmmm mmmmm."

"Hmmmmmmmmmmmmmmmmmmmm mmmmmmmmmmmmmmmm," Gabrielle hummed.

"Good," Lydia Jane said. "Now listen sharp, and try to find your way around the room. Flap your arms like wings."

Gabrielle did as she was told. Lydia Jane did the same. Pretty soon they were bumping into things. Hmmmmmmmmmmmmm mmmmmmmmm BUMP! In another minute they bumped into each other. They laughed and fell down. Then they got up and tried again.

Hmmmmmmmmmmm BUMP!

Hmmmmmmmmmmmmmmmmmmmmmm mmmmmmmmmmmmmmmmmm BUMP!

CRASH!

"Good heavens! Whatever is going on in here?" Mrs. Humphrey said.

Two bats stopped in midflight.

"We're bats!" Gabrielle said.

"We're using our sonar," Lydia Jane said. She thought that sounded more official.

Mrs. Humphrey waggled a dish towel at them. "Now, you girls know how I feel about roughhousing."

"It wasn't roughhousing," Lydia Jane said. "It was practice."

"Anything that makes such a racket is roughhousing," Mrs. Humphrey said. "And when children roughhouse, someone gets hurt. So I expect you to find something quiet . . . and *safe* . . . to do." She turned on her heel and walked out.

Lydia Jane sank down on the floor and leaned back against the sofa.

"I don't like her," Gabrielle said. She sat down next to Lydia Jane.

Lydia Jane picked up the remote control to the TV. She punched the buttons for channel 14.

"Are we going to watch the weather?" Gabrielle asked.

"No," Lydia Jane said, "we're watching the little numbers at the bottom of the screen."

"What for?" Gabrielle asked.

"Because they tell the time," Lydia Jane said. "You see it says four-oh-three right now. Well, when it says five-one-five, it's time to go."

"Home?" Gabrielle said.

"Yes, home," Lydia Jane said.

Gabrielle sighed and leaned against Lydia Jane. "Let's watch, then," she said.

Lydia Jane considered for a while, then said, "Something special is going to happen when we leave today, Gabrielle."

"What?"

"It's kind of a surprise. So if I tell you, you have to keep it a secret," Lydia Jane said.

"Okay," Gabrielle said, "I will."

"But you have to promise," Lydia Jane said. Gabrielle had a way of accidentally telling people what was in a gift right before they opened it. "This surprise might not happen if you talk about it too soon."

"Okay, promise," Gabrielle said.

"It's called an au pair," Lydia Jane said.

"What's au pair?"

"It's like a baby-sitter exchange. It means when we leave Mrs. Humphrey's today, we're not coming back."

"Ever?" Gabrielle asked.

"Ever," Lydia Jane said.

"I like this surprise," Gabrielle said.

"But you can't tell anybody yet," Lydia

Jane reminded her. "Not even Mrs. Humphrey."

"Okay," Gabrielle said. She leaned her head against Lydia Jane's arm and gazed into the distance. "Au pair," she whispered.

Chapter

4

As soon as Lydia Jane woke up on Saturday morning, she knew it was going to be a wonderful day.

First, she could hear the sounds of hammering. That meant her parents were already up and working in the garage. Working on Lydia Jane's room. By the end of the day, the room would be one day closer to completion. It wouldn't be too many more weekends before her parents said, "Moving day!" and Lydia Jane would have a room of her own.

Next was the raccoon print experiment. Lydia Jane had gone out the evening before, right after supper. She had soaked and smoothed the mudflat again. There would not have been enough time for the mud to dry and harden before dark when the raccoons came out. This morning she'd find prints for sure.

And finally, this was the day to tell her parents about the au pair. Lydia Jane had gone to sleep thinking about her brave au pair the night before. She had thought of several more things to tell her parents to look for when they were getting the au pair.

The au pair should not be afraid of a little dirt.

She should leave her shoes in the living room like a real person.

She should like new games.

She should not think that noisy was the same thing as dangerous.

She should have wavy, blond hair that reached in a braid to her waist.

Lydia Jane threw back the covers and hopped out of bed. She stripped off her nightie and pulled on her baggy red pants and her orange striped shirt. She found two socks and her shoes and put these on as well.

In the kitchen, Lydia Jane poured herself a bowl of cereal. While she ate, Gabrielle danced through the room. She flapped her arms and hummed "Row, Row, Row Your Boat."

"I'm a bat!" she said.

Lydia Jane thought of reminding her to close her eyes and hum just one note. Then she changed her mind; Gabrielle seemed happy.

"I'm a bat with a secret," Gabrielle said. "Is it time to tell?"

"Not yet," Lydia Jane said. "I'll let you know when."

At the end of breakfast, Lydia Jane left her empty bowl on the table and ran out the side door. She ran around the house to the mudflat by the crawl space hole. Her eyes grew large, and her jaw dropped.

There were footprints. Big ones. Running in both directions past the crawl space entry.

There was only one thing wrong. The footprints weren't raccoon prints. They were people prints. Someone with big sneakers had walked through Lydia Jane's experiment.

"Dad!" Lydia Jane said aloud.

She steamed back into the house and through the laundry room passage to the garage.

"Dad!" she called.

Mr. Bly was hammering a nail into a piece of wallboard. Mrs. Bly was measuring off another piece of Sheetrock that lay across a pair of sawhorses.

"Lydia Jane," her father said, "come take a look. We should have the rest of this wallboard up by tonight."

"Dad, you walked in my experiment!" Lydia Jane said.

"I don't know how," her father said. "I've been right here since six A.M."

"But you did, though," Lydia Jane said. "Look at your shoes!" She pointed an accusing finger. Her father's shoes were streaked with dried mud.

Mr. Bly looked at his shoes. Lydia Jane's

mother looked, too. "Ohhh . . ." they both said at once.

"So you're the one who's turned our backyard into a wallow," Mr. Bly said.

"Your father slipped in that mud when he took out the garbage last night," her mother said. "And you left the hose right where he could trip over it."

"It must be an experiment in breaking necks," Mr. Bly said. He pulled a nail from his belt pouch and resumed hammering.

"It's not," Lydia Jane said. "It's an important experiment about the raccoons. How was I supposed to know you'd take out the trash in the dark?"

"You need to think of these things," her mother said. "And anyway, what kind of an experiment is it that calls for making a swamp?"

"It was just a puddle," Lydia Jane said. She explained how she was going to learn about the raccoons from their prints. "It would have worked, too, if somebody hadn't tromped in it."

"Well, good," her father said. "I hope it

does work. Because as soon as I know how many raccoons we have under the house, I'm going to call County Pest Control to come trap them."

"You wouldn't do that!" Lydia Jane said.

Her father whammed another nail into the wall. "I would," he said. "Especially if they keep waking me up at night."

Lydia Jane turned and stormed out of the garage room. She didn't know why her parents had to be so cranky about a little mud. And about the raccoons, who weren't hurting anybody as far as Lydia Jane could tell.

And now she would have to wait to tell them about the au pair. There was no sense wasting a perfectly good idea on cranky parents.

Lydia Jane used the hose and the piece of two-by-four and smoothed away her father's prints. Then she pulled the benches from the picnic table and made a barricade around her mudflat. That way nobody could tromp through by accident.

For the rest of the morning, Lydia Jane played with Gabrielle. She knew that her parents got annoyed if Gabrielle pestered them when they were working. If Lydia Jane wanted happy parents, playing with Gabrielle would help.

Lydia Jane and Gabrielle played bats until they had bumps all over. Then they watched a column of ants as it traveled between the garden and the house.

"You have to pay attention to how ants walk," Lydia Jane said. "If they're zigging and zagging, they're going *away* from their home. If they're going straight, they're going *back* to their home. You can tell where they live from how they walk."

Gabrielle studied the ants for a while. Then she said, "I want to be an ant."

"We can do that," Lydia Jane said. "Follow me." They went out to the sidewalk and zigged and zagged their way single file to the end of Washoe Court. Then they scurried back home in a straight line.

At lunchtime, when their parents called them in, Gabrielle showed them how she could be an ant. Their parents talked about how close they were to finishing the walls in the garage room.

"This sandwich is great," Lydia Jane said. Her mouth was full of white bread, bologna, and cheese.

Her mother smiled.

"I have an idea," Lydia Jane said. "I could clean my room today. I could even clean Gabrielle's side."

Now both her parents smiled. Her parents were in very good moods, she realized. This was just the right moment.

"I have another idea, too," Lydia Jane said. "This one is even better. It's about a new kind of sitter called an au pair."

"It's a secret," Gabrielle said.

Mrs. Bly raised one eyebrow. "Who do you know who has an au pair?" she asked.

"Juliet Fisher's cousins," Lydia Jane said. "I don't know them exactly, but I know Juliet. She told me how the au pair lives at her cousins' house and her aunt and uncle can go anyplace they want without worrying. So I think we should get one. That way you'd never have to worry we weren't safe. And the au pair could take us everywhere. Like to the San Francisco Exploratorium, and even to the dentist."

Mrs. Bly gasped. Lydia Jane could tell her mother was stunned by what a terrific idea this was.

"Let me get this straight," Mr. Bly said. "We'd get an au pair to live here? Right in this house?"

"Yes!" Lydia Jane said. "And she could even drive me to school. I'd always be on time."

"We don't have to go back to Mrs. Humphrey's!" Gabrielle said.

"I guess she'll drive your car," Mr. Bly said to his wife. He was grinning a big grin. Lydia Jane could tell he liked the idea, too.

"Not *my* car," Mrs. Bly said. "I need mine to get to work."

"Well, of course I need mine, too," Mr. Bly said, "even though it's in the shop half the time."

"Maybe we could get an au pair who already has a car," Lydia Jane said quickly. This was not a good time to have her parents start arguing about cars. "Juliet says au pairs come in all kinds."

"Wonderful!" Mr. Bly said. "Maybe she'd drive me to work."

"Juliet's cousins' au pair is even pretty. She's from Finland."

"I'd like that!" Mr. Bly said. His grin had grown larger.

"Roger!" Mrs. Bly said. She scowled. Then she turned to Lydia Jane.

"Dear heart, I don't think you've thought this through all the way," she said. "For instance, an au pair is customarily provided with a room of her own. Have you thought about where we'd *put* an au pair?"

"Oh," Lydia Jane said. She hadn't thought of that.

And now that she did think about it, she realized it was a problem. A big one.

Lydia Jane looked down at her half-eaten sandwich. She poked a finger through the bread to the bologna. There was really only one answer to the problem of where to put the au pair. And Lydia Jane didn't much like it. She had looked forward to her new room for such a long time.

Still, if the au pair needed a room of her own . . .

"I guess we could give her my room,"

Lydia Jane said. "I don't mind sharing with Gabrielle."

"I like sharing," Gabrielle said. "I'll share my cookie." She broke a cookie in two and shoved half over to Lydia Jane.

"There's just one thing," Lydia Jane added quickly. "I want a very brave au pair."

"Why not?" her father said. "Let's get one that cooks while we're at it." His grin had turned into a soft chuckle.

"Now Roger, stop that," Mrs. Bly said. "You know perfectly well it's out of the question."

"But why?" Lydia Jane asked. "Why is it out of the question if I give her my room?"

"Because we can't afford an au pair, dear. You have to pay them as well as house them."

"Don't you pay Mrs. Humphrey?" Lydia Jane asked.

"Yes, but not nearly so much. And we don't pay taxes and insurance for her. Or house and feed her and buy gas for her car. An au pair is a very expensive proposition."

"A rich person's proposition," Mr. Bly

said. He stood up and got a soft drink from the refrigerator. "But if I could afford it, I'd get an au pair in a heartbeat. A pretty one at that. And a swimming pool and a sailboat. And maybe a summer house at Lake Tahoe.

"In fact, I'd *give* her that miserable car of mine, and buy one with a little style." He popped the top of his soft drink and winked at Lydia Jane.

"Then we can't have an au pair?" Lydia Jane asked.

"Not unless you can get yourself adopted by a couple of big-city lawyers with even bigger incomes," her father said.

"Your friend's cousins probably live in Marin County," Mrs. Bly said.

Lydia Jane shoved away the plate with the remainder of her sandwich. She had suddenly lost her appetite. "No brave au pair," she said, and shook her head.

"Is the secret over?" Gabrielle asked.

"It's over," Lydia Jane said.

"Au pair!" Gabrielle hollered. "I don't have to go back to Mrs. Humphrey's. I can be a bat!" She got up and zoomed around the table with her arms flapping.

Mrs. Bly caught Gabrielle up in her arms on the second pass. "You can be a bat at home," she said. "But you do have to go back to Mrs. Humphrey's."

"But Lyddie said . . ."

"I know," their mother said. "But she shouldn't have told you that without checking first. We can't get an au pair. And we need both you girls to make the best of things with Mrs. Humphrey." She gave Lydia Jane a hard look.

Lydia Jane groaned. "Okay," she said. "But you could have told us sooner." She looked at her father. She had an idea he had teased her some about the au pair. And Lydia Jane did not like to be teased when she was talking about something serious. Maybe adoption wasn't such a bad idea.

When her parents went back to work on the garage, Lydia Jane played ants a while longer with Gabrielle. She thought Gabrielle needed some cheering up.

Later she went into her room and thought about her offer to clean it.

"Maybe not," she said. After all, it wasn't really so bad. And who was coming to see it? No one. Most especially not a pretty and brave au pair.

That night, as Lydia Jane lay in her bed, she heard the raccoons begin their nightly snarling and fighting. She remembered what her father had said about how they kept him awake.

"Have babies," she whispered. "Breed."

And then she fell asleep.

Chapter

5

*L*ydia Jane sat on Juliet Fisher's front steps and tugged at the laces of one roller skate.

"I'm ready," Juliet said from the doorway. "Now if I can just figure out how to get down the steps."

Lydia Jane turned to look at her friend. Her eyes popped. Juliet was wearing elbow pads and knee pads. She had on shin guards and wrist braces. On her head was a helmet with a face mask and a plastic chin cup. And on her feet were a pair of brand-new skates.

"Good grief, Juliet. Is that you in there?" Lydia Jane said.

Juliet edged her way cautiously along the railing. Then she sat and scooted down the steps one at a time.

"It's me," Juliet said. "At least I think it's me. These are my first skates." She stuck out a foot. "My grandmother in Arizona sent them for my birthday."

"She must expect you to crash a lot," Lydia Jane said.

"No," Juliet said. "My grandmother just gave me the skates. My mother bought the padding. She says no child of hers is going to end up in the emergency room with broken bones. Of course there's not much chance of that. How can I fall down if I can't even stand up?"

"Come on," Lydia Jane said. "I'll help." She stood and held out her hands.

Juliet clutched the railing and eased herself to her feet. One at a time she reached out a hand to Lydia Jane. "Whoooaaa . . ." she said.

Lydia Jane skated slowly backward.

"Whooooaaaa . . ." Juliet said again.

Lydia Jane guided Juliet down the front walk, to the sidewalk and past two more houses. At the third house, the sidewalk began to slope gently downhill.

"I'm letting go," Lydia Jane said. "You keep going."

"Whoooaaaaa!" Juliet called. "How do I stop?"

"Aim for something soft," Lydia Jane hollered.

Juliet wobbled on down the sidewalk, gaining speed as she went. "WHOOAAAA!" she yelled. Then, "*Hellllppp . . .*" Then at last she veered off to the right, across a short stretch of parking strip, and landed hard on her bottom.

"Ow!" she yelled.

"Are you okay?" Lydia Jane asked when she rolled up.

"I don't know," Juliet moaned.

"It's all the fault of gravity," Lydia Jane said. "If you ask me, we have way much more gravity on Earth than we need. But it's hard to do anything about it."

"There's more gravity than *I* need," Juliet said. "I'm sure of that."

"People need feathers," Lydia Jane said. "Anything that will push against the air slows you down. Like a parachute. Or feathers. Birds have it lucky, because feathers really slow them down when they land."

"Well, I don't have feathers," Juliet said. "So I guess I need a parachute."

"Except they don't open if you're too near the ground," Lydia Jane said. "I know, 'cause I've tried it." Lydia Jane scratched her head.

"You need something that's lighter than air," she said. "Like a hot air balloon. Or helium. If we could get you attached to a big helium balloon, you could fall and never get hurt."

"Except I don't happen to have a helium balloon," Juliet said. She stood up and rubbed her bottom. "But I just got an idea for a new constellation. We can call it The Bruised Skater."

"We can put it where I was going to put my Brave Au Pair," Lydia Jane said. "I found out I'm not getting one."

"Why not?" Juliet asked.

"Because they cost lots of money. And they

need their own rooms," Lydia Jane said. She sighed. "I guess we need the kind of sitter you get if you have just enough money but no extra."

"Huh," Juliet said. "It sounds like that's what you've already got."

Lydia Jane thought about that. "I guess you're right," she said.

"Anyway," Juliet said, "maybe you'll get to go back to Happy Times Day Care. Mindy says that brat Acey is moving to New Jersey. I think that's a long way away."

"Wherever it is, it probably won't matter. I don't think my mother would let us go back to Happy Times anyway. She says it's the grown-up's job to pay attention to the kids. Nobody pays much attention to anything at Happy Times." Lydia Jane sighed again. "That's why I liked it."

Juliet clomped carefully back to the sidewalk. She pointed herself toward Manzanita Street, in the downhill direction. "Just give me a shove," she said. "A small one. I don't want to land too hard."

Lydia Jane snapped her fingers. "I've got

it," she said. "You need an umbrella. It will work like a parachute except better. It's already open to catch the air."

"My dad has an umbrella he uses when he plays golf," Juliet said. "Three people can fit under it. It's in the garage with his clubs."

"What are we waiting for?" Lydia Jane said.

Lydia Jane held on to Juliet's arm, and they made their way slowly back to Juliet's house. In the garage they found a large green-and-white umbrella.

"Perfect!" Lydia Jane said. "Now, you just hold it open behind you when you go forward. That will create drag. And then, when you're about to fall, hold it over your head."

Juliet swung the umbrella above her head. "Like this?" she asked.

"Right," Lydia Jane said. "It's antigravity."

Juliet and Lydia skated their way from one end of Tehema Street to the other, and then back. Sometimes Lydia Jane supplied a small push to help Juliet get started. Once Juliet skated into a bush. Several times she fell. Soon the spokes of the umbrella were bent in odd shapes.

As Lydia Jane and Juliet skated up and down Tehema Street, they noticed that it seemed to make people happy to see them skate. Several neighbors stopped to watch. One even took a picture of Juliet. When they were both tired and hungry, they skated home to Juliet's house.

They left their skates and Juliet's padding on the steps. Then they got snack food and went upstairs to Juliet's room.

"Your room is getting awesome," Lydia Jane said.

"I know," Juliet said. "It's starting to look like yours. I can't find anything anymore." She laughed. "My schoolbooks are under my clothes somewhere."

"You need some jars of mold," Lydia Jane said.

"I was thinking of that," Juliet said.

Lydia Jane gobbed cream cheese onto a cracker. She put an olive on top. She put another cracker on top and handed it to Juliet. Then she made one for herself.

"I can't believe I'm learning to skate," Juliet said with a mouth full of cracker.

"I told you—anybody can skate," Lydia Jane said.

"Yeah, but I've had those skates for a whole month," Juliet said. "I just kept looking at them. The worst part was my mom kept saying I had to write Grandma a thank-you note. And all I could think of to say was, 'Thanks for the skates.' Nothing else."

"Now you can say, 'Thanks for the skates, I'm joining the Roller Derby,'" Lydia Jane said.

"Or I can say, 'Thanks for the skates, Dad's golf umbrella is shaped like a chicken,'" Juliet said. They both laughed.

"Tell her you want Rollerblades next time," Lydia Jane said. "That's what I want."

Juliet furrowed her brow. "I'd better not ask for Rollerblades," she said. "My grandmother is like my mom. She worries. If I told her I wanted Rollerblades, she'd probably come all the way from Arizona just to give me a lecture."

Lydia Jane smeared cream cheese on more crackers. Juliet put olives on top.

"My grandmother never worries," Lydia Jane said. "My mother's mother, that is. Everyone says I take right after her. Once I was visiting her in Walnut Creek and a tarantula was walking across the road we were driving on. Right across the road!

"Grandma stopped the car and turned on her flashers. Then she got out and stopped the cars that were coming from the other direction. Pretty soon there were all these cars parked in the road and everyone was out watching the tarantula cross the street. I think my grandma is absolutely great."

"Except for the part about the tarantula," Juliet said. "Tarantulas are icky." She shuddered.

"They're not, really," Lydia Jane said. "Maybe you just have to get used to them. I've seen lots of tarantulas because they live all around Walnut Creek. Mostly they live on Mount Diablo in burrows, and they come out more at night than in the day. But sometimes they come out in the day. Like the one that crossed the road. My grandmother loves them."

"Your grandmother sounds like the kind of person who would let you out in the hail," Juliet said.

"She would," Lydia Jane said. "In fact, she'd be out there, too. She's very brave."

Lydia Jane picked up a cracker and got it halfway to her mouth. Then she stopped. She blinked. She blinked again. She set the cracker back down.

"Juliet?" she said. "You know what?"

"What?"

"You just saved my life. My whole, entire life! You're wonderful. You're amazing!" Lydia Jane flung her arms around Juliet. "I have to go," she said.

Then she was down the stairs and almost out the door while Juliet called after her, "What did I do? Lydia Jane?"

Lydia Jane got halfway down the block before she realized she'd left her high tops on Juliet's front steps. She ran back and grabbed her shoes. But she didn't stop to put them on. She ran all the way home in her socks.

She streaked through the kitchen and out the laundry room to the garage. "Hi!" she said.

"Goodness, Lydia Jane. You startled me," her mother said.

Gabrielle was pounding nails into a piece of scrap lumber. "I'm building, Lyddie," she said.

"This room is sure great," Lydia Jane said.

"Well, I'm glad you think so," her father said. He was troweling putty-colored stuff onto a wall in great, sweeping strokes. "As soon as I'm done mudding this wall, that's it for the day," he said. "I'm skunked."

Lydia Jane leaned against the doorjamb and caught her breath. "I bet when Grandma sees this room, she'll completely love it," she said.

Mrs. Bly pushed a lock of hair out of her eyes. "Your grandma?" she said. "Why, what made you think of Grandma just now?"

"Juliet was talking about her grandmother," Lydia Jane said. "So I got to thinking about mine. Ours." She looked at Gabrielle.

"Well, I was just thinking of her myself," Mrs. Bly said. "I really should give her a call. It's been almost a month since we talked."

"I bet she misses us," Lydia Jane said.

"Yes, I imagine she does," her mother said. She picked up a trowel and a bucket of goop. She smeared a streak across the wall.

"Do you think she's lonely in Walnut Creek?" Lydia Jane asked.

"Maybe," Mrs. Bly said. "I know she misses your grandpa since he died. But I don't know if she's really lonely. She doesn't say so."

"I'll bet she is," Lydia Jane said. "I'll just bet."

Lydia Jane walked back through the cottage. She squirmed under her bed where she knew there was a nearly full package of fresh binder paper. Then she got a pencil from her backpack. She moved aside piles of folded clothes and plopped on her bed.

Lydia Jane had a letter to write.

Chapter

6

Dear Grandma,

Please come to live at our house. If you do, you won't have to be lonely. You can even have the new room in the garage. It's very big, and I will put glow-in-the-dark stars on the ceiling for you. We don't have any tarantulas, but we have raccoons. And I can show you where to find banana slugs. When it hails, we can go outside together and catch some.

If you live here, we won't need a sitter. Now we have to go to Mrs. Humphrey's and she's *very terrible. She doesn't let us do anything at all, so I can't find out how things work. And if I can't find out how anything works, I'll never be able to figure out how to patch the hole in the ozone layer.*

So hurry up and pack!

Your granddaughter who is just like you,
Lydia Jane Bly

P.S. If a meteorite lands, we'll keep it.

Lydia Jane had a lot to do on Monday morning. And she needed to do it quickly if she wanted to get to school in time for sharing. Which today, for a change, she did.

She moussed her hair into a series of spikes and swirls and finished dressing. Then she got an envelope and a stamp from her parents' desk in the living room. She carefully printed her grandmother's address on the envelope and sealed the letter inside. She stuffed the letter into the left-hand pocket of her yellow parachute pants.

Next Lydia Jane took a spatula from the kitchen drawer. She grabbed a Ziploc bag and her books and lunch box, and left the house. Out back, she moved aside the bench barrier and kneeled beside the mudflat.

It was still there.

One perfect raccoon pawprint.

Lydia Jane used the edge of the spatula and sliced a large, deep square around the pawprint. Then, gently, she eased the spatula under the print and lifted it. Finally, she put the entire block of dried mud, print and all, into the Ziploc bag. She stuck the bag into the right-hand pocket of her pants.

Lydia Jane jogged all the way down Washoe Court and two blocks up Yolo Avenue to the nearest mailbox. She dropped her letter into the box and let the door go with a clang. Then she turned back toward school.

By the time she saw the pale green stucco of Mills Elementary School, Lydia Jane was out of breath. She had a stitch in her side, and her face felt hot. There were no other children in sight, so she supposed she had missed the bell. She drew in great gulps of air, and in a final burst, ran the rest of the way.

"Did I miss sharing?" she asked as she fell into her seat by Juliet.

"Not yet," Juliet said.

"Thank goodness," Lydia Jane said. She leaned forward and rested her cheek on the cool desktop.

"How many people have something to share?" Mrs. Lacey asked.

Lydia Jane shot her hand into the air. So did a half dozen other kids.

"We only have time for about three today," Mrs. Lacey said.

Lydia Jane waved her hand madly. So did everyone else.

"Granville," Mrs. Lacey said.

Juliet groaned. "I bet it's something about war," she said.

Granville stood in the front of the room. He held up an army-green case. "I got this at the surplus store," he said. "It's called an entrenching tool. It's like a shovel except it folds up. If you want to make a foxhole, you just unfold it and dig." He showed how to unfold the entrenching tool.

"It's for war," Juliet said. "I knew it."

"Who would like to be next?" Mrs. Lacey asked.

Lydia Jane waved her hand madly again. So did everyone else.

"Sara," Mrs. Lacey called.

"It's about someplace she went with her family," Juliet said. "They never stay home."

"This weekend we went to Marine World," Sara said. "It was my third time. I sat in the front row at the killer whale show. When they jumped, I got completely soaked." She sat down.

"Told you," Juliet said.

Lydia Jane shot her hand into the air. She got on her knees on her seat.

"Who would like to be last?" Mrs. Lacey asked.

"Me!" Lydia Jane said. Four other kids waved their hands and said, "Me!"

Mrs. Lacey looked at Lydia Jane. Her eyes twinkled. "I suppose we'd better find out why Lydia Jane came early today," she said.

"Yes!" Lydia Jane said.

"All right!" said Juliet.

Lydia Jane stood by Mrs. Lacey's desk at the front of the room. "We have raccoons living under my house," she said. "We've never seen them, but we know they're there 'cause we can hear them. And if we forget to put cinder blocks on top of the trash cans, they tip them over and make a big mess. All night long they snarl and fight and find things to eat, like garbage. All day long they sleep. That's because they're nocturnal. Anybody can be nocturnal. All you have to do is sleep all day and stay up all night. Try it sometime."

Mrs. Lacey made a small noise like something had caught in her throat.

"Anyway," Lydia Jane said, "I made an experiment to find out about the raccoons. I wanted to know how big they are and how many there are. So I made a footprint experiment. See, that's one of the ways the scientists found out about trilobites and dinosaurs. They found prints in mud. Some prints were millions of years old. Mine is one day old. I dug it up."

She reached into her right-hand pocket and pulled out the Ziploc bag. "This is the print of a big raccoon," she said.

"Uh-oh," someone said.

"No, it's not," came another voice.

Lydia Jane stared bleakly at her Ziploc bag. It was filled with loosely piled dirt.

"I don't believe it," she said. "It took me days to get this footprint. Now it's dust."

"I'm very sorry," Mrs. Lacey said. "It was an unusual thing to share."

Lydia Jane walked slowly back to her seat. Then she turned. "Mrs. Lacey," she asked, "can I have the rest of my turn another day?"

"Of course," Mrs. Lacey said.

"Good," Lydia Jane said. "'Cause I'm going to bring a pawprint to school. I just don't know how."

Juliet patted her shoulder. "Maybe if you didn't put it in your pocket next time," she said. "You could pack it in cotton balls. Or those little Styrofoam squiggles."

"Maybe," Lydia Jane said. "But I think it should be hard like a fossil."

"That would work," Juliet said.

Lydia Jane sighed. "The only trouble is, it takes about a million years to make a fossil. I'll be out of third grade by then."

"Probably," Juliet said.

For the rest of the morning, Lydia Jane

stared at her bag of dirt and thought. Mrs. Lacey read the class a story, but Lydia Jane didn't hear it. Then Mrs. Lacey handed out worksheets about the story. Lydia Jane drew a line of raccoon prints around the edge and left the rest blank.

"Are you sick?" Juliet asked at last.

"No," Lydia Jane said. "Do I look sick?"

"Well, you've been really quiet. Usually you talk all the time."

"I talk most of the time," Lydia Jane said. "Except when I'm thinking." She poked at the bag of dirt. "There's a way to make it hard like a fossil," she said. "I just don't know what it is yet. But I know how to find out."

"How?" Juliet asked.

"At the Westmont Public Library. There's a place called the Reference Desk and a lady who helps you find out anything you want to know. She helped my dad figure out how to fix up the electricity for my new room. If she can't find out something herself, she calls the San Francisco Public Library. I'm going there after school."

Except during recess and lunch, Lydia

Jane watched the clock for the rest of the day. Sometimes it seemed the minute hand had become stuck. It didn't move at all.

At last the 2:30 bell rang. Lydia Jane streaked out of Mills Elementary School. Often she dragged her feet all the way to Mrs. Humphrey's house. Today she ran.

Lydia Jane punched the doorbell. Twice.

"Why, Lydia Jane!" Mrs. Humphrey said. Her eyebrows arched higher than ever over her glasses. "I didn't realize it was that time already."

"I might be early," Lydia Jane panted. "I'm in a hurry. I need to go to the library, but I wanted to tell you so you'd know where I was."

"To the public library?" Mrs. Humphrey asked.

Lydia Jane nodded.

"Why, Lydia Jane, that's blocks from here!"

"Yeah, but I know the way," Lydia Jane said. "I've been lots of times."

"Surely not on your own!" Mrs. Humphrey said. Her eyebrows disappeared into her hair.

"It's no big deal," Lydia Jane said. "Sometimes I ride my bike there on Saturdays. And it's even farther from my house than it is from here. My parents don't mind."

Mrs. Humphrey folded her hands under her apron. "Well," she said, "if your parents let you wander around on your own, that's their business. But as long as I'm responsible for you, you'll stay where I know you're safe." She stood aside in the doorway.

"But . . ."

"No buts," Mrs. Humphrey said. "Come on in now."

"It's not fair," Lydia Jane said.

"In," Mrs. Humphrey said.

Lydia Jane edged past Mrs. Humphrey. "You're ruining a very important experiment," she said. "I hope you know that."

Mrs. Humphrey's eyebrows suddenly flopped down. "My job is to look after you, and that's exactly what I intend to do," she said. She pulled the door closed. "Now, how about that snack?"

"No, thanks," Lydia Jane said. "I'm not hungry."

Lydia Jane marched into the den and sat down hard on the flowered sofa.

"Lyddie!" Gabrielle said. "Let's play. I've waited and waited."

"Not right now," Lydia Jane said. "I'm not in the mood."

"Are you mad?" Gabrielle asked.

"Very mad," Lydia Jane said.

Gabrielle's lower lip drooped.

"But not at you," Lydia Jane said. "At Mrs. Humphrey."

Gabrielle sighed. "Okay," she said. She sat on the sofa and watched Lydia Jane closely.

Lydia Jane wished she could walk right out of Mrs. Humphrey's house and never come back. She'd go straight home. No, she'd go to the library, then straight home.

She thought about the letter she had mailed to her grandmother that morning. Mail didn't get where it was going the same day, Lydia Jane knew that much. But she wasn't sure exactly how long it would take. And then of course her grandmother would have to pack. How long would that take? A day? Two? Then it was about a two-hour drive from Walnut Creek. Her grandmother probably wouldn't arrive in time to keep Lydia Jane from having to go back to Mrs. Humphrey's tomorrow.

Gabrielle leaned against Lydia Jane and punched the channel selector on the remote control. News. Commercials. Cartoons. Talk show. Commercials . . . Lydia Jane wished she could tell Gabrielle that Grandma was coming. But she knew her parents would get mad again if she told Gabrielle something before it happened. Just in case it didn't happen.

Only Lydia Jane knew her grandmother wouldn't let her down.

"I have an idea," Lydia Jane said. "Let's be bears."

"Bears growl!" Gabrielle said. "We can growl at Mrs. Humphrey." She turned off the TV.

"Sometimes they growl," Lydia Jane said. "Other times they don't make any noise at all. Like when it's winter and they go into caves to hibernate. We're going to be hibernating bears. Cinnamon bears, because they have red hair."

"Yea!" Gabrielle said.

"Shhhh," Lydia Jane said.

She pulled the sheet from the sofa. She and Gabrielle crawled under the sheet and curled up into balls. They closed their eyes.

Some while later two cinnamon bears heard footsteps outside their cave.

"Heavens!" Mrs. Humphrey said. "*Now* what are you up to?"

Nobody answered. Hibernating bears don't talk.

Chapter

7

*L*ydia Jane stood at the kitchen sink with a potato peeler in her hand. Gabrielle stood on a chair beside her. A colander full of carrots and potatoes sat in the sink.

Gabrielle held up a carrot. "This one next," she said.

"Okay," Lydia Jane said. She reached for the carrot.

Gabrielle pulled it away. "No," she said, "this time a potato." She handed Lydia Jane a potato instead.

"Are you sure?" Lydia Jane asked.

Gabrielle giggled. "No! A carrot!" She snatched the potato back.

Lydia Jane laughed.

"Girls," their mother said, "if we're going to get to the library tonight, I need you to help without fooling around."

"Well, it's not my fault we have to go on a Thursday night," Lydia Jane said. "If it wasn't for Mrs. Humphrey, I could have gone after school today. Or yesterday. Or the day before. So blame her, not me."

"I'm not blaming anyone," Mrs. Bly said. "Mrs. Humphrey's just doing what she thinks is right. And when you're at her house, you have to follow her rules."

"Even if they're stupid?"

"Even if you *think* they're stupid," her mother said.

Mrs. Bly opened and closed several high cupboards. Then she squatted down and opened and closed the low cupboards. "Roger?" she called.

Mr. Bly came in from the garage. He was carrying a pad of paper and a pencil. "I think two gallons of paint will do it," he said.

"Have you seen my big iron skillet?" Mrs. Bly asked. "The heavy one?"

Lydia Jane and Gabrielle looked at each other.

"About yo big?" Mr. Bly said. "Black?"

"That's the one," Mrs. Bly said.

"Haven't seen it," Mr. Bly said. "Not unless it's the one that's upside down in the backyard."

"In the backyard?" Mrs. Bly said. "Why on earth would my skillet be out there?"

For a moment the only sound in the room was the peeler scraping against a carrot. Then Lydia Jane felt her parents' eyes on her.

"I needed it to cover something up," she said.

"Lyddie caught a footprint!" Gabrielle said.

"My good skillet?" Mrs. Bly said.

"Two prints," Lydia Jane said. "Anyway, it had to be heavy or the raccoons might tip it over."

"Raccoons are walking in my skillet?" Mrs. Bly said. "The one I was going to bake our red snapper in?"

"Not *in* it," Lydia Jane said. "*On* it. Or maybe they'll walk around it, I don't know."

"*In* is fine by me," Mr. Bly said. "Maybe instead of calling Pest Control, we should just eat them. I wonder what raccoon tastes like."

"Dad!" Lydia Jane said.

"I don't want that for dinner," Gabrielle said with a scowl. "I never, ever eat raccoons."

Mrs. Bly shook her head. "My skillet. In the yard."

"Sunk about a half inch deep in mud when I saw it last," Mr. Bly said.

Lydia Jane's mother gave a little squeak.

"Well, blame Mrs. Humphrey," Lydia Jane said. "If she'd let me go to the library when I wanted to, I'd already have figured out how to fossilize the raccoon prints and I wouldn't need to keep them covered up."

"I think I'm hearing another complaint about Mrs. Humphrey," Lydia Jane's father said.

"Never mind," Mrs. Bly said. "I'll bake the snapper in my lasagna dish. But Lydia Jane, I wish you'd ask before you do these things."

Lydia Jane wondered whether she should mention that her mother had already left for work this morning when she'd found the prints. Or that looking for the skillet had made Lydia Jane late to school again. She decided not to.

Mr. Bly picked up a peeled carrot from the drainboard and bit into it. "I need to know what color you want your room painted," he said to Lydia Jane.

"Do you have to know right now?" Lydia Jane asked.

"Right now would be good," he said. "I want to pick up the paint on the way home from work tomorrow so I can get it done this weekend. The carpet is coming next Wednesday."

"Well . . ." Lydia Jane hesitated. "It's just that I thought I'd ask Grandma what color she likes."

Mrs. Bly squeezed fresh lemon all over the red snapper. "Why do you need to ask Grandma?" she said.

"In case she wants to stay in my room sometime," Lydia Jane said.

"That's very thoughtful of you," her father

said, "but this is your room. And when your grandmother comes, she sleeps on the sofa bed, as you know."

"But in case," Lydia Jane said. She kept her head bent over the potato she was peeling. She didn't want her parents to guess about her grandmother until she actually arrived.

"Well, your grandmother would choose white," Mrs. Bly said. "She's always painted everything white. But you'll probably want a little color."

"No," Lydia Jane said quickly. "I want white. I was just thinking of that. White would be perfect."

Mr. Bly shrugged. "Suits me," he said. "White is easiest to get anyway."

"Except one thing," Lydia Jane said. "I want the ceiling black."

"Black!" her parents both said at once.

"Yeah," Lydia Jane said. "Like space. I'm going to put my glow-in-the-dark stars up there, and I think it should be black like space, don't you?"

"I don't know . . ." her mother said.

"Not a chance," her father said. "A black ceiling would be awful. Anyway, with the lights out, it will *look* black, and that's close enough. We're painting the walls white, so we'll do the ceiling the same."

"Okay, fine," Lydia Jane said. "But I don't know why you asked if you were going to do the choosing."

Mr. Bly took a large knife from the rack and began slicing potatoes. "Have you noticed the change in our girls lately?" he said to his wife. "Lydia Jane has been grumpy for days. And Gabrielle isn't exactly gabby."

"I've noticed," Mrs. Bly said. She dropped the potato slices into sizzling canola oil.

"I don't think they're our girls at all," Mr. Bly said. "I think they've been swapped."

"Well, I hope they get swapped back," Mrs. Bly said. "I liked the others better."

After dinner, while Mr. Bly washed dishes, Lydia Jane and Gabrielle climbed into the backseat of their mother's two-door Ford.

"We have less than an hour," Mrs. Bly said as she fastened her seat belt. "So choose your books quickly, Lydia Jane. I'll help Gabrielle."

"You should get her extras," Lydia Jane said. "So she'll have something to do at Mrs. Humphrey's besides watch TV."

Lydia Jane ran up the steps of the Westmont Public Library two at a time. She walked quickly past the checkout desk and turned left. She walked down a short hall and turned left again. She stopped in front of a desk with a sign that said REFERENCE.

"Ahem," she said.

A woman with short blond hair turned around. "May I help you?" she asked.

"Yes," Lydia Jane said. "I need to make a fossil, quick. I want to find out how."

"You want to make a fossil?" the woman asked. "Goodness, I don't think anyone has ever made a fossil. I think they make themselves."

"Well, I want to make one," Lydia Jane said.

"Hmmmm," the woman said. "Maybe you should tell me why you need to make a fossil. Perhaps then I can help."

Lydia Jane explained about the raccoons under her house. She explained about the footprint experiment and about how the print fell apart when she dug it up. All the while, the woman at the reference desk listened closely.

"So it needs to be hard, like a fossil," Lydia Jane said at last. "And it has to be fast, because my mom wants her skillet back."

"Ahhh," said the woman, "I think I know what you want. I think you need to find out how to take an *impression*. It's different from a fossil. But you can take an impression of a fossil if you're a scientist. Or you can take an impression of teeth if you're a dentist. You can even take an impression of tire tracks if you're a detective. Let's find out how it's done."

"Let's!" Lydia Jane said. She knew she had come to the right place.

For the next thirty minutes the reference librarian looked on computer files. She looked on microfilm and in books. Lydia Jane looked with her.

"There are several things you can use to

take impressions," she said at last. "But as near as I can tell, plain plaster of paris will work for your raccoon prints. Why don't you try that?"

"Where do I get plaster of paris?" Lydia Jane asked.

"At the hardware store, I believe," said the woman.

The lights in the reference room flicked twice. It was closing time.

"Thanks!" Lydia Jane said. "I'll let you know how it works."

"I hope you do," said the woman. "I hope you'll bring your impression by and show it to me!"

Lydia Jane settled happily into the backseat of her mother's car. Gabrielle sat opposite her. In between was a pile of picture books almost as high as Gabrielle's head.

Mrs. Bly backed slowly out of the parking space.

"Can we go to the hardware store?" Lydia Jane asked.

"The hardware store is closed," Mrs. Bly said. She turned on her blinker and pulled into the road.

Lydia Jane groaned. "I'll bet Mrs. Humphrey won't let me go to the hardware store after school tomorrow," she said.

"Probably not," her mother said.

Lydia Jane watched as trees and houses went by the car window. If Mrs. Humphrey wouldn't let her go to the hardware store, she'd have to wait until Saturday. She sighed. Mrs. Humphrey sure could slow things down. It seemed that all Lydia Jane did lately was wait.

Lydia Jane had waited all week for her grandmother as well. Though she kept that waiting to herself. In her mind she got a picture of her grandmother's condominium in Walnut Creek. Two walls in the living room were lined floor to ceiling with books. Then there were other shelves and cases. These were full of mineral samples and small animal skeletons and birds' nests— things that her grandma loved. And that Lydia Jane loved, too. There were other closets and cupboards full of dishes and clothes and all manner of things.

Whew. The more Lydia Jane thought about it, the more it seemed her grandmother had a lot of stuff to pack. She hoped it would all fit in the garage room.

"Mom?" Lydia Jane asked.

"Yes?" Mrs. Bly said.

"How old was I when we moved into our house?"

Mrs. Bly turned east on Yolo Avenue. "You were two," she said. "Why?"

"Because I don't really remember it," Lydia Jane said. "I almost remember it, but not quite. And I was wondering . . . did it take you a long time to pack?"

"Not too long," her mother said.

"But *how* long?" Lydia Jane asked.

"Maybe three days," Mrs. Bly said. "We didn't own so many things as we do now." She signaled to turn left onto Washoe Court.

Lydia Jane thought. "Well, how long would it take to pack if we moved now?"

Her mother laughed. "We're not going to move, thank goodness."

"But *if*," Lydia Jane said.

"Weeks. I hate to think of it." Mrs. Bly pulled into the drive and turned off the engine. "Two weeks, anyhow."

Lydia Jane looked over at Gabrielle. She was sound asleep. The pile of books had slid into her lap.

Two weeks was a long time. Two more weeks of Mrs. Humphrey was a very long time. She and Gabrielle had hibernated for three days already. You'd have to be a *real* bear, Lydia Jane figured, to last for two weeks.

Chapter

8

*L*ydia Jane *looked at her watch. She* looked at the circular white form in front of her, then she looked at her watch again.

"Hi!" came a voice.

Lydia Jane started. "Juliet! I didn't know you were coming," she said.

"Well, I telephoned. But your mom said you were stuck out here or something, so I just came over. Do you want to skate? You left yours at my house. I brought them." Juliet was wearing all her padding. Lydia

Jane's skates were tied together and hung over her shoulder.

"I'm not stuck, exactly," Lydia Jane said. "I'm guarding my experiment. As soon as this plaster of paris is dry I can see if it worked."

Juliet knelt on the ground beside Lydia Jane. She studied the cardboard collar that Lydia Jane had fashioned and filled with plaster of paris. "I think it's dry," she said.

"Well, it *looks* dry," Lydia Jane agreed, "but it might be wet at the bottom."

"How long is it supposed to take?" Juliet asked.

"About fifteen minutes, I think," Lydia Jane said.

"How long has it been?" Juliet asked.

"About two hours."

"It's dry," Juliet said.

Lydia Jane shook her head. "I don't know. If this doesn't work, I'll have to start all over."

"It's dry," Juliet said. "Trust me."

Lydia Jane gingerly touched the surface of

the plaster of paris. It was firm. She pushed harder. It was solid.

"Okay," she said. "Here goes."

Juliet sat cross-legged to watch.

Lydia Jane dug under the plaster of paris, and under the mud. She lifted up the mud-covered mold and peeled off the cardboard collar. She chipped and brushed the mud from the bottom of the plaster of paris. Two perfect raccoon prints, one slightly forward of the other, appeared in relief on the bottom of the plaster.

"Awesome," Juliet said.

"Fantastic!" Lydia Jane said. "It actually worked. I *hoped* it would work, but I wasn't sure till now. I can't wait to take it to school." She sat back on her heels and gazed at the impressions.

"So, do you want to skate?" Juliet asked.

There was no answer.

"Lydia Jane? Earth to Lydia Jane," Juliet said.

"Huh?" Lydia Jane said. "I was thinking."

"I said, do you want to skate? I'm getting good at antigravity."

"Sure, I guess," Lydia Jane said.

Juliet loosened and retied the lace on one skate.

Lydia Jane watched. All at once her eyes got large. "Hold it!" she said.

"What?" Juliet asked.

"If I can make raccoon print impressions," she said, "I can make impressions of other animal footprints. Right?"

"Right," Juliet said. She loosened the lace on the other skate.

"And people are a kind of animal," Lydia Jane said. "Right? I mean, we're mammals and all that, right?"

"I guess . . ." Juliet said.

"And you're a kind of people!" Lydia Jane said.

"Well . . ." Juliet said.

"Take off your skates. Take off your socks, too!" Lydia Jane said. "I'll have a whole collection of prints. You'll be my first *Homo sapiens!*"

Juliet hesitated. "Is this going to hurt?" she asked.

"No way," Lydia Jane said. "In fact, it will feel good. Did you ever walk through mud in your bare feet?"

"No," Juliet said. "But I've walked through mud with my shoes on."

"This will feel better than that," Lydia Jane said.

Juliet considered. "Okay," she said at last. "Let's do it. And *after*, we'll skate."

Lydia Jane ran for the hose. In a jiffy she had made another mudflat. Juliet set her right foot firmly in the mud. Then she lifted it up. She left behind an exact Juliet Fisher footprint.

"Wow," Lydia Jane said. "This is going to be great. I'm going to be able to get foot-prints of all kinds of animals."

"As long as you can get them to come to your house," Juliet said.

Lydia Jane thought. "Well, it's true we don't have too many big wild animals around here. But there are plenty of rac-coons. And plenty of people." Then she said, "Wait here."

Lydia Jane ran into the house and looked for Gabrielle. She found her in the garage room.

"I'm glad you're here," Mrs. Bly said.

"Gabrielle has been helping us paint. But she's getting bored. She's started to paint things that aren't the walls."

"I painted that by myself," Gabrielle said. She pointed at a streaked area low on one wall.

"That's very good," Lydia Jane said.

"And she painted that," Mr. Bly said, pointing to the bottom three rungs of the stepladder he was on. "I think I'm stuck up here until it dries."

"Come on," Lydia Jane said to Gabrielle. "I have something for you to do out back."

Gabrielle set down her paintbrush. Lydia Jane unbuttoned the old shirt Gabrielle had been wearing for a smock and helped her out of it. She led her to the bathroom and washed paint from Gabrielle's hands. Then they went outside.

"See?" Lydia Jane said. "I got prints of the raccoons." She showed her the plaster of paris impression. "And now I'm going to get prints from Juliet and from you," she said. "You just put your foot in the mud right by Juliet's."

Gabrielle looked doubtful. "If I play in mud, Mommy gets mad," she said.

"She won't this time," Lydia Jane said. "You'll just stick your foot in, and then we'll rinse it off. Mom won't mind."

"Okay," Gabrielle said.

Lydia Jane unlaced Gabrielle's shoes and took them off. She rolled up Gabrielle's coveralls. Then she helped her into the mud. "You can put both feet in," she said, "but don't wiggle your toes."

Gabrielle squealed. "It's cold," she said.

Lydia Jane lifted her out. "Look," she said. "Gabrielle prints."

Gabrielle squatted and inspected the footprints. "Those feet are mine," she said.

"Can we go skating now?" Juliet asked. Her skates were already on. She was busy lacing the last one.

Lydia Jane looked at the footprints in the mud. "The mud has to dry first," she said. "Then I have to mix the plaster of paris and wait for that to dry."

Juliet groaned. "We get to skate next week, right?" she said.

"Well," Lydia Jane said, "I suppose the mud can dry by itself. Or maybe Gabrielle would watch it for me. And keep Dad from tramping in it. Would you do that, Gabrielle?"

Gabrielle was still staring intently at her footprints. "I'll watch it," she said.

Lydia Jane put on her skates and laced them snugly. She and Juliet clomped down the path by the house, and out to Washoe Court.

"And now," Juliet said, "The Amazing Juliet Fisher, Roller Derby Queen, is about to knock your socks off." She pushed off in long, even strokes down the sidewalk.

"Hey," Lydia Jane yelled, "wait for me!"

One behind the other, Lydia Jane and Juliet skated to the end of Washoe Court. They turned the corner and skated east down Yolo Avenue. At the next corner, Juliet came to a stop under a tree.

"Pretty good, huh?" she said.

"You can really skate!" Lydia Jane said.

"Well, I can't do anything fancy yet," Juliet

said. "But I practiced every day after school this week."

"I guess you won't need the antigravity umbrella anymore," Lydia Jane said.

Juliet laughed. "It's a good thing I don't," she said. "My dad says I can't use it again. I guess it's sort of bent."

Juliet pushed off from the tree. "Follow me," she called. "It's eleven blocks, and there's a surprise at the end. I know you like surprises."

This was true. Lydia Jane liked almost any kind of surprise.

They turned through the neighborhood streets. Right and then left, right and then left again. After a time Lydia Jane called, "Do you know where you're going?"

"Completely," Juliet called back.

At last they turned onto Sacramento Avenue. "We're here," Juliet said.

The Iceman's!" Lydia Jane said.

"Yeah," Juliet said. "I thought now that I can skate, I should skate to someplace special. Next I thought of ice cream. And then I thought that since you taught me to skate it would be fun if we *both* ate ice cream.

Like a celebration. So my mom said she'd treat if I helped her clean house this afternoon."

"I like any celebration that has ice cream," Lydia Jane said.

"That's what I thought," Juliet said. "What's your favorite kind of giant sundae?" She pushed open the door to The Iceman's.

Lydia Jane had a giant peppermint sundae with hot fudge sauce. Juliet had a giant banana sundae with butterscotch sauce. When they were done, they skated slowly home holding their stomachs.

At Yolo Avenue, Lydia Jane turned right, and Juliet went straight.

"See you in school on Monday," Juliet called. "Bring your raccoon print."

"I'm bringing yours, too!" Lydia Jane called in return. "Good-bye."

Lydia Jane skated the rest of the way home thinking about how much plaster of paris she would need to mix for her people prints. And thinking about other places she could get animal prints. There might be some in the woods behind her cottage if she looked carefully. And she could ask friends to bring over their pets. The neighbors two doors down had a dog. And Jonah Twist was always talking about his kitten, Mrs. Einstein. There was even someone who had a rabbit for a pet, if she could just remember who.

With all this on her mind, Lydia Jane never noticed the white Toyota in her driveway until she was standing right beside it.

Lydia Jane blinked. The car looked very familiar. Whose . . . ? And then she knew.

Lydia Jane half ran and half stumbled to the steps. She tore off her skates. "Grandma!" she yelled as she burst through the door.

"In here," came a voice from the living room.

Lydia Jane's grandmother was seated on the sofa. On her lap, in fresh clothes, and with her hair still damp from a bath, was Gabrielle. Lydia Jane flung herself on this heap and gave her grandmother three big kisses.

"I knew you'd come!" she said.

"I'll always come if you really need me," her grandmother said. "You know that." She hugged Lydia Jane tight.

"Young lady," Mrs. Bly said.

Lydia Jane turned. She hadn't noticed her mother seated in the armchair. Her voice did not sound friendly.

"I understand you told Gabrielle that I wouldn't mind if she played in mud," her mother said. "And to be sure to keep your father away. I can't imagine what you were thinking of."

"It wasn't playing," Lydia Jane said. "I was just making a footprint. That's all."

"Well, Gabrielle threw a fit when your father tried to get her out of that puddle," Mrs. Bly said.

"*Out* of it," Lydia Jane said. "Oh, no. She wasn't supposed to get *in*. She was just supposed to *watch* it." Then she had another thought. "Are my people footprints all messed up?" she asked.

"I don't know anything about footprints," her mother said. "But there's a very clear impression of Gabrielle's body, if that's what you're wondering."

Lydia Jane moaned. "Gabrielle, what did you do?"

"I made a print of me!" Gabrielle said. "You can keep it, Lyddie."

"But . . ." Lydia Jane began.

"From now on . . ." her mother said.

"Now, now," her grandmother said. "Children are bound to get into trouble from time to time. Even when there are very responsible adults nearby." She looked hard at Mrs. Bly.

"I don't need a lecture, Mother," Mrs. Bly said.

"No?" Lydia Jane's grandmother said. "I thought perhaps you did. But in any case, it's a very nice day, and I'd like to take my two granddaughters someplace, if that's all right with everyone."

Lydia Jane's mother sank back in her chair. "That would be lovely," she said.

"Where are we going?" Gabrielle asked.

"I thought perhaps to the Academy of Sciences in Golden Gate Park," her grandmother said. "And while we're there, we can fill up on hamburgers and burritos."

Lydia Jane didn't feel hungry. But she knew that could change. "Can we go to the planetarium, too?" she asked.

"I was thinking of that," her grandmother said. "And if we leave right now, we might make it just in time for the first show."

Late that afternoon, as they drove south on the freeway out of the city, Lydia Jane said, "Today was the most fun I've had in ages and ages. But every day will be fun now that you're here, Grandma."

Her grandmother looked thoughtful at the wheel of the car. "Lydia Jane," she said, "there's something we need to talk about. I won't be staying."

"You won't be staying?" Lydia Jane said. "But Grandma, you *have* to stay. Didn't you see your room? Don't you like it?"

"It's a marvelous room," her grandmother said, "but it's yours. Your parents have worked very hard to make it for you, and you'll be glad to have it someday."

"I'm glad already," Lydia Jane said. "But I don't mind sharing with Gabrielle if it's for you. Honest, I don't."

"It's not because of the room, though," her grandmother said. "There are other reasons." She brushed a lock of silver and pale red hair from her forehead. "You see, Lydia

Jane, I have a life of my own that I like very, very much. If I left Walnut Creek, I'd miss my life there. And even though I miss your grandad, I'm not really lonely."

"But don't you miss *us*?" Lydia Jane asked. She had a lump in her throat. She was glad Gabrielle was asleep in the backseat in case she cried. Sometimes if Lydia Jane cried, Gabrielle cried, too. Even if there was no reason.

"Of course I miss you," her grandmother said. "And I think maybe I'll try to come visit you more often—since we miss each other. But it's really best if I live my own life. And best if you and your parents live your own lives. You'll understand that more when you're older."

Lydia Jane looked down at the small fish fossil she held in her hand. Her grandmother had bought it for her in the Academy of Sciences gift shop. She swallowed.

"You don't understand," she said. "When we're with you, we do things that are interesting. And you're brave. But Mrs. Humphrey is just the opposite. She's really, really awful, Grandma. The only thing she doesn't mind is TV. She thinks everything else is dangerous."

Lydia Jane's grandmother furrowed her brow. "TV is about the only thing I think *is* dangerous," she said. Then she said, "Mrs. Humphrey is probably a perfectly nice person. But that doesn't necessarily mean she's the best person to look after small children."

"She's not," Lydia Jane said. "So please stay, Grandma. We really need you a bunch."

Lydia Jane's grandmother signaled for the Westmont exit ramp. "That's just why I came," she said. "Because you needed me. And I will help, I promise you that. But then, after I've helped, Lydia Jane . . . then I'll go."

Her grandmother reached out a hand and patted Lydia Jane on the knee. "One more thing, dear," she said. "I wouldn't worry too much about the hole in the ozone layer if I were you. I'm sure you'll have it all worked out by the time you're grown."

Chapter

9

*L*ydia Jane walked along a path through the woods. She was holding the hand of a girl. The girl had long black hair that reached past her shoulders in a braid.

"Over there," Lydia Jane said, "is a place where you can find banana slugs. And down that bank by the creek is where my grandma and I found the deer print. I made an impression of it. But it's at school right now with my other prints."

"Is this the same grandmother you named the constellation in your room for?" the girl asked.

"The Brave Grandma," Lydia Jane said. "That's the one. You'll meet her because she's going to come spend the night in my room sometime. We're going to look at the constellations and listen to the raccoons fight."

"I'd like to see those raccoons," the girl said.

"I'd like to see them myself," Lydia Jane said. "I keep trying. But so far the only way I know they're there is from their pawprints and the fighting. But my dad says they can stay. Grandma told him rats won't move into a house that has raccoons, and that did it."

Lydia Jane spotted a very black rock and stooped to pick it up. She turned it over in her hand. She shook her head. "Nope," she said. "Too many sharp edges. Grandma says meteorites are black and rounded off from burning as they come through the earth's atmosphere. This is definitely not a meteorite."

"You're lucky to have a grandmother who knows about such interesting things," the girl said.

Lydia Jane tossed the rock back on the ground. "I know," she said. "But mostly what my grandma does is help. She helped find a preschool for Gabrielle. She said Gabrielle's brain was turning into goo from too much TV at Mrs. Humphrey's. Which I could have told my parents if they'd have listened.

"Now Gabrielle goes to this place called Steppingstone, where they do all kinds of neat things. When she comes home, she never shuts up. We call her 'Gabby' now."

They walked along in silence for a minute. Then Lydia Jane said, "In a way, my grandma is the reason you're here. She told my parents, 'Find a lively high school girl to look after Lydia Jane.' I guess that's you."

"I guess it is." The girl laughed.

"But I thought you'd have blond hair, though," Lydia Jane said.

"Do you mind?" the girl asked. She tugged at her braid.

Lydia Jane considered. "Not really," she said. Then she asked, "Have you tried hibernating?"

"No," the girl said, "have you?"

"Yes," Lydia Jane said.

"Is it fun?"

"Actually, it's boring," Lydia Jane said. "I don't know how bears stand it when there's so much else to do."

"Look!" the girl said. "Up there! There's a nest at the very top of that old dead tree. What do you suppose lives there?"

"Ravens," Lydia Jane said. "I've seen them."

Lydia Jane had a question she'd been wanting to ask. All at once, this seemed the moment to do it.

"What would you do if it hailed?" she asked.

"*Now*, you mean?"

"Right now," Lydia Jane said.

The girl laughed again. "That's easy," she said. "I'd hold out my hands and catch some."

"I knew it!" Lydia Jane said. "I absolutely knew it."